Modern Love

Modern Love

GEORGE MEREDITH

Edited by GILLIAN BEER

SYRENS

GEORGE MEREDITH 1828–1909

S Y R E N S Published by the Penguin Group. Penguin Books Ltd, 27 Wrights Lane, London w8 5tz, England. Penguin Books USA Inc., 375 Hudson Street, New York, New York 10014, USA. Penguin Books Australia Ltd, Ringwood, Victoria, Australia. Penguin Books Canada Ltd, 10 Alcorn Avenue, Toronto, Ontario, Canada m4v 3b2. Penguin Books (NZ) Ltd, 182–190 Wairau Road, Auckland 10, New Zealand. Penguin Books Ltd, Registered Offices: Harmondsworth, Middlesex, England. Published in Syrens 1995. Preface, narrative and notes copyright © Gillian Beer, 1995. All rights reserved. The moral right of the editor has been asserted. Except in the United States of America, this book is sold subject to the condition that it shall not, by way of trade or otherwise, be lent, re-sold, hired out, or otherwise circulated without the publisher's prior consent in any form of binding or cover other than that in which it is published and without a similar condition including this condition being imposed on the subsequent purchaser. Set in 9.5/12pt Monotype Bembo by Datix International Limited, Bungay, Suffolk. Printed and bound by Page Bros., Norwich.

PREFACE

'When I entered the world again, I found that one had quitted it who bore my name: and this filled my mind with old melancholy recollections which I rarely give way to.'

So wrote George Meredith halfway through a paragraph in a letter to his friend William Hardman at the end of October 1861. It is the only surviving reference to the death of his estranged wife Mary. The following April, 1862, the fifty-poem sequence *Modern Love* was published; it is a passionate analysis of a foundering relationship, the ending of a marriage. The sequence sets itself at odds with Victorian poetic idealizations of domestic life, such as Coventry Patmore's *The Angel in the House* (1854–62), and it brings into question too the courtly tradition of the Renaissance sonnet.

The brilliant Mary had borne other names before Meredith's: that of her father Thomas Love Peacock, the satirical novelist and friend of Shelley, and that of her first husband, a young naval officer named Edward Nicolls, who died only months after their marriage. She never bore the name of her lover, the painter Henry Wallis, for whom she left Meredith and who in turn left her. The marriage between Mary and George lasted several years, through cramped housing, several miscarriages, the care of two young children and the career uncertainties of two ambitious literary people. The events of the poem are not identical with their lives: in the poem the husband tries to involve himself with another woman, as the wife has done with another man. When at last they speak fully to each other, misunderstanding – or a too full understanding – leads the wife to suicide.[1] But though the events differ, the experience of the marriage is packed and shaken into the language of the poem. The lines flinch and quiver with the ricochet of moods that seize people

---

1 See 'Narrative' below, p.xi, for a fuller account of the poem's action.

in such crisis: arch, rancorous, sensual, barren, tender, desolate. Yet though the poem may be generated out of a particular marriage, it is not locked to that personal experience; indeed, it sounds very immediate across nearly one hundred and fifty years.

No wonder contemporary reviewers were shocked by the poems, 'absurdly called "Modern Love"', as one wrote. The poems scotch the domestic idyll and undo the home as a place of refuge. Here the extremest reaches of suffering are experienced in the domestic space. The poems display a married couple walking together, entertaining their friends, laughing at domestic jokes, sharing a bed, while beneath the surface shrieks of rage, jealousy, desolation issue silently like wraiths, the more excruciating for being mingled with old tenderness and desire. The poetic line lies so close to the husband that he sometimes becomes 'I'; then the narrative seems to move eerily closer still when 'I' again becomes 'he'. The distance implied is that of schizophrenic splitting rather than judicious surveillance. Throughout, the sequence suggests that intimacy survives alienation; painfully, drawing apart does not uncouple the married pair from each other.

Between is a keyword in the sequence, signifying at once connection and separation: rupture, choice, split, and wedge – the conjunction keeps the parted lovers together, but barely:

> Like sculptured effigies they might be seen
> Upon their marriage-tomb, the sword between;
> Each wishing for the sword that severs all.

So ends the first sonnet. The estranged couple lie on their marriage bed, each pretending to sleep, she stifling her sobs to lie 'stone-still'. Yet they are not quite dead; the sword between them recalls the great lovers Tristan and Isolde as well as the marmorealized married couples of medieval tombs. Tristan and Isolde long to make love; the 'sculptured effigies' represent a couple who have fulfilled a married life. The couple of *Modern Love* are painfully caught between these possibilities, in a present elongated through a night that seems endless. 'Where came the cleft between us? whose the fault?' (VIII:4); 'League-sundered by the silent gulf between' (XXII:14); 'Time leers between us, twiddling his thumbs' (XXXIV:4).

Yet it would be misleading to present these as gloomy poems: they are exhilarated, witty, mordant. Meredith freely invents compound words, often at odds within themselves, and a great many words appear only in *Modern Love* and nowhere else in his large œuvre. While he was writing the sequence Meredith referred to it as 'A Love-Match', a title with a typical ironic clash: true union, game, and competition. There is pleasure in the play of wit, an intimacy renewed between husband and wife like surface tension as they keep their secret from their friends. The delight in wit is also a symptom of the marriage breakdown: the husband evades the wife's intermittent attempts at utterance, dreading what will come out. The reader is given an enticing and disturbing set of roles: straining to hear the wife's voice past the husband's self-pity, sharing his chagrin, spying on them both, questioning, colluding, caught into a drama more secret than any we could watch on stage or in the life of any of our friends.

The poems in *Modern Love* are often described as sonnets, though in fact they are sixteen lines long, not fourteen, and composed in four quatrains. They have neither the emphatic turn of octave and sestet nor the summary ending of the alternative sonnet form. Rather, their form outgoes, literally, the containing sonnet which it also uses: instead of fourteen lines, producing crisis, musing, resolution sometimes, here we have a surplus that refuses to be curtailed, the beat of thought and rhyme continuing past expected limits.

The effect favours narrative episodes linked onward and backward within and past each poem. This allows, as a Victorian commentator, J.W. Marston, well observed, the story to be 'rather hinted at than told ... These sonnets resemble scattered leaves from the diary of a stranger. The allusions, the comments, the interjections, all refer to certain particulars which are not directly related, and have to be painfully deduced.' The reader, never acknowledged, becomes in that process an intimate.

Present-day readers are more used than their Victorian counterparts to marriage breakdown as a subject for literature. But *Modern Love* still surprises with the honesty of its insight and its excoriating precision. What comfort it offers comes from the poem's sustained passion and invention.

Gillian Beer

NARRATIVE

In *Modern Love* a married couple, grown distant, try
to find a way to speak truly to each other, yet dare
not begin. Much of the action takes place in the
husband's mind beneath the surface of domestic
events; it follows the twists and turns of his moods
and interpretations, ranging from lust, to forgiveness,
to sardonic pleasure, violent jealousy, and remorseful
recollection of his own failings in the relationship.
The wife's speech is from time to time recorded, but
for much of the sequence her feelings remain enig-
matic. The wife, 'Madam', loves another man,
though she is not his mistress. The husband attempts
to fall in love with another woman, 'Lady'. Each
partner observes the other's love affair from afar.

They conceal their unhappiness from their friends and take a certain joint pleasure in doing so. Eventually, the married couple draw together again, but without an equal renewal of love. In that anguished intimacy they question each other with clinical intensity and for a little while they reach serenity. The husband fears that he now pities his wife more than he loves her. The wife believes the husband to love his woman friend and wishes to free him. But when they meet on the shore she comes to feel her husband's love for her again; but she doubts her own power to return it or to renew their married relationship. That night, she drinks poison, then calls him to her for a clarifying kiss.

Modern Love

This is not meat
For little people or for fools.
Book of the Sages[2]

---

2 This epigraph is Meredith's invention.

I

By this he knew she wept with waking eyes:
That, at his hand's light quiver by her head,
The strange low sobs that shook their common bed
Were called into her with a sharp surprise,
And strangled mute, like little gaping snakes,
Dreadfully venomous to him. She lay
Stone-still, and the long darkness flow'd away
With muffled pulses. Then, as midnight makes
Her giant heart of Memory and Tears
Drink the pale drug of silence, and so beat
Sleep's heavy measure, they from head to feet
Were moveless, looking thro' their dead black years,
By vain regret scrawl'd over the blank wall.
Like sculptured effigies they might be seen
Upon their marriage-tomb, the sword between;
Each wishing for the sword that severs all.

II

It ended, and the morrow brought the task:
Her eyes were guilty gates that let him in
By shutting all too zealous for their sin:
Each suck'd a secret, and each wore a mask.
But, oh the bitter taste her beauty had!
He sicken'd as at breath of poison-flowers:
A languid humour stole among the hours,
And if their smiles encounter'd, he went mad,
And raged, deep inward, till the light was brown
Before his vision, and the world forgot,
Look'd wicked as some old dull murder spot.
A star with lurid beams,[3] she seem'd to crown
The pit of infamy: and then again
He fainted on his vengefulness, and strove
To ape the magnanimity of love,
And smote himself, a shuddering heap of pain.

---

3 *A star with lurid beams*: allusions to the fallen angel Lucifer, 'the
light-bearer', are attached to the wife throughout the sequence.

III

This was the woman; what now of the man?
But pass him! If he comes beneath our heel
He shall be crush'd until he cannot feel,
Or, being callous, haply till he can.
But he is nothing: – nothing? Only mark
The rich light striking from her unto him:
Ha! what a sense it is when her eyes swim
Across the man she singles, leaving dark
All else! Lord God, who mad'st the thing so fair,
See that I am drawn to her even now!
It cannot be such harm on her cool brow
To put a kiss? Yet if I meet him there!
But she is mine! Ah, no! I know too well
I claim a star whose light is overcast:
I claim a phantom-woman in the Past.
The hour has struck, though I heard not the bell!

IV

All other joys of life he strove to warm,
And magnify, and catch them to his lip:
But they had suffered shipwreck with the ship,
And gazed upon him sallow from the storm.
Or if Delusion came, 'twas but to show
The coming minute mock the one that went.
Cold as a mountain in its star-pitch'd tent
Stood high Philosophy, less friend than foe:
Whom self-caged Passion, from its prison-bars,
Is always watching with a wondering hate.
Not till the fire is dying in the grate,
Look we for any kinship with the stars.
Oh, wisdom never comes when it is gold,
And the great price we pay for it full worth.
We have it only when we are half earth.
Little avails that coinage to the old!

V

A message from her set his brain aflame.
A world of household matters fill'd her mind,
Wherein he saw hypocrisy design'd:
She treated him as something that is tame,
And but at other provocation bites.
Familiar was her shoulder in the glass
Through that dark rain: yet it may come to pass
That a changed eye finds such familiar sights,
More keenly tempting than new loveliness.
The 'What has been' a moment seem'd his own:
The splendours, mysteries, dearer because known,
Nor less divine: Love's inmost sacredness,
Call'd to him, 'Come!' – In that restraining start,
Eyes nurtured to be look'd at, scarce could see
A wave of the great waves of Destiny
Convulsed at a check'd impulse of the heart.

VI

It chanced his lips did meet her forehead cool.
She had no blush, but slanted down her eye.
Shamed nature, then, confesses love can die:
And most she punishes the tender fool
Who will believe what honours her the most!
Dead! is it dead? She has a pulse, and flow
Of tears, the price of blood-drops, as I know
For whom the midnight sobs around Love's ghost,
Since then I heard her, and so will sob on.
The love is here; it has but changed its aim.
O bitter barren woman! what's the name?
The name, the name, the new name thou hast won?
Behold me striking the world's coward stroke!
That will I not do, though the sting is dire.
– Beneath the surface this, while by the fire
They sat, she laughing at a quiet joke.

VII

She issues radiant from her dressing room,
Like one prepared to scale an upper sphere:
– By stirring up a lower, much I fear!
How deftly that oil'd barber lays his bloom!
That long-shank'd dapper Cupid with frisk'd curls,
Can make known women torturingly fair;
The gold-eyed serpent dwelling in rich hair,
Awakes beneath his magic whisks and twirls.
His art can take the eyes from out my head,
Until I see with eyes of other men;
While deeper knowledge crouches in its den,
And sends a spark up: – is it true we're wed?
Yea! filthiness of body is most vile,
But faithlessness of heart I do hold worse.
The former, it were not so great a curse
To read on the steel-mirror[4] of her smile.

4 *steel-mirror*: literally, a mirror made of steel, as well as her smile's steely reflection; compare V:6–7 'Familiar was her shoulder in the glass/Through that dark rain'.

VIII

Yet it was plain she struggled, and that salt
Of righteous feeling made her pitiful.
O abject worm, so queenly beautiful!
Where came the cleft between us? whose the fault?
My tears are on thee, that have rarely dropp'd
As balm for any bitter wound of mine:
My breast will open for thee at a sign!
But, no: we are two reed-pipes, coarsely stopp'd:[5]
The God once filled them with his mellow breath;
And they were music till he flung them down,
Used! used! Hear now the discord-loving clown
Puff his gross spirit in them, worse than death!
I do not know myself without thee more:
In this unholy battle I grow base:
If the same soul be under the same face,
Speak, and a taste of that old time restore!

---

5 *reed-pipes, coarsely stopp'd*: Pan-pipes.

IX

He felt the wild beast in him betweenwhiles
So masterfully rude, that he would grieve
To see the helpless delicate thing receive
His guardianship through certain dark defiles.[6]
Had he not teeth to rend, and hunger too?
But still he spared her. Once: 'Have you no fear?'
He said: 'twas dusk; she in his grasp; none near.
She laughed: 'No, surely; am I not with you?'
And uttering that soft starry 'you', she lean'd
Her gentle body near him, looking up;
And from her eyes, as from a poison-cup,
He drank until the flittering eyelids screen'd.
Devilish malignant witch! And oh, young beam
Of Heaven's circle-glory! Here thy shape
To squeeze like an intoxicating grape –
I might, and yet thou goest safe, supreme.

6 *defiles*: narrow places.

X

But where began the change; and what's my crime?
The wretch condemn'd, who has not been arraign'd,
Chafes at his sentence. Shall I, unsustain'd,
Drag on Love's nerveless body thro' all time?
I must have slept, since now I wake. Prepare,
You lovers, to know Love a thing of moods:
Not like hard life, of laws. In Love's deep woods
I dreamt of loyal Life: – the offence is there!
Love's jealous woods about the sun are curl'd;
At least, the sun far brighter there did beam. –
My crime is that, the puppet of a dream,
I plotted to be worthy of the world.
Oh, had I with my darling help'd to mince
The facts of life, you still had seen me go
With hindward feather and with forward toe,
Her much-adored delightful Fairy Prince!

XI

Out in the yellow meadows where the bee
Hums by us with the honey of the Spring,
And showers of sweet notes from the larks on wing,
Are dropping like a noon-dew, wander we.
Or is it now? or was it then? for now,
As then, the larks from running rings send showers:
The golden foot of May is on the flowers,
And friendly shadows dance upon her brow.
What's this, when Nature swears there is no change
To challenge eyesight? Now, as then, the grace
Of Heaven seems holding Earth in its embrace.
Nor eyes, nor heart, has she to feel it strange?
Look, woman, in the west. There wilt thou see
An amber cradle near the sun's decline:
Within it, featured even in death divine,
Is lying a dead infant, slain by thee!

XII

Not solely that the Future she destroys,
And the fair life which in the distance lies
For all men, beckoning out from dim rich skies:
Nor that the passing hour's supporting joys
Have lost the keen-edged flavour, which begat
Distinction in old time, and still should breed
Sweet Memory, and Hope, – Earth's modest seed,
And Heaven's high-prompting: not that the world is
    flat
Since that soft-luring creature I embraced,
Among the children of Illusion went:
Methinks with all this loss I were content,
If the mad Past, on which my foot is based,
Were firm, or might be blotted: but the whole
Of life is mixed: the mocking Past must stay:
And if I drink oblivion of a day,
So shorten I the stature of my soul.

XIII

'I play for Seasons; not Eternities!'
Says Nature, laughing on her way. 'So must
All those whose stake is nothing more than dust!'
And lo, she wins, and of her harmonies
She is full sure! Upon her dying rose
She drops a look of fondness, and goes by,
Scarce any retrospection in her eye;
For she the laws of growth[7] most deeply knows,
Whose hands bear, here, a seed-bag; there, an urn.
Pledged she herself to aught, 'twould mark her end!
This lesson of our only visible friend,
Can we not teach our foolish hearts to learn?
Yes! yes! – but oh, our human rose is fair
Surpassingly! Lose calmly[8] Love's great bliss,
When the renew'd forever of a kiss
Sounds thro' the listless hurricane of hair!

7 *the laws of growth*: perhaps Darwin's recent *Origin of Species*
(1859) reinforces the view here of nature as demanding change.
8 *Lose calmly*: not a command, rather, 'It is impossible to lose
calmly.'

XIV

What soul would bargain for a cure that brings
Contempt the nobler agony to kill?
Rather let me bear on the bitter ill,
And strike this rusty bosom with new stings!
It seems there is another veering fit,
Since on a gold-hair'd lady's eyeballs pure,
I look'd with little prospect of a cure,
The while her mouth's red bow loosed shafts of wit.
Just Heaven! can it be true that jealousy
Has deck'd the woman thus? and does her head
Whirl giddily for what she forfeited?
Madam! you teach me many things that be.
I open an old book, and there I find
That 'Women still may love whom they deceive.'
Such love I prize not, Madam: by your leave,
The game you play at is not to my mind.

XV

I think she sleeps: it must be sleep, when low
Hangs that abandon'd arm towards the floor:
The head turn'd with it.⁹ Now make fast the door.
Sleep on: it is your husband, not your foe!
The Poet's black stage-lion¹⁰ of wrong'd love,
Frights not our modern dames: – well, if he did!
Now will I pour new light upon that lid,
Full-sloping like the breasts beneath. 'Sweet dove,
Your sleep is pure. Nay, pardon: I disturb.
I do not? well!' Her waking infant stare
Grows woman to the burden my hands bear:
Her own handwriting to me when no curb
Was left on Passion's tongue. She trembles thro';
A woman's tremble – the whole instrument: –
I show another letter lately sent.
The words are very like: the name is new.

9 *low hangs . . . The head turn'd with it*: Henry Wallis, Mary
Meredith's lover, portrayed Meredith in just such a pose when
Meredith acted as model for his picture 'The Death of Chatterton'.
10 *The Poet's black stage-lion*: Othello.

XVI

In our old shipwreck'd days there was an hour,
When in the firelight steadily aglow,
Join'd slackly, we beheld the chasm grow
Among the clicking coals. Our library-bower
That eve was left to us: and hush'd we sat
As lovers to whom Time is whispering.
From sudden-open'd doors we heard them sing:
The nodding elders mix'd good wine with chat.
Well knew we that Life's greatest treasure lay
With us, and of it was our talk. 'Ah, yes!
Love dies!' I said: I never thought it less.
She yearn'd to me that sentence to unsay.
Then when the fire domed blackening, I found
Her cheek was salt against my kiss, and swift
Up the sharp scale of sobs her breast did lift: —
Now am I haunted by that taste! that sound!

XVII

At dinner she is hostess, I am host.
Went the feast ever cheerfuller? She keeps
The Topic over intellectual deeps
In buoyancy afloat. They see no ghost.
With sparkling surface-eyes we ply the ball:
It is in truth a most contagious game;
HIDING THE SKELETON shall be its name.
Such play as this the devils might appal!
But here's the greater wonder; in that we,
Enamour'd of our acting and our wits,
Admire each other like true hypocrites.[11]
Warm-lighted glances, Love's Ephemerae,[12]
Shoot gaily o'er the dishes and the wine.
We waken envy of our happy lot.
Fast, sweet, and golden, shows our marriage-knot.
Dear guests, you now have seen Love's corpse-light[13]
    shine!

---

11 *hypocrites*: acting a part on stage, so feigning, pretending.
12 *Love's Ephemerae*: winged insects that live for a day only.
13 *Love's corpse-light*: also called a 'corpse-candle', a flaming exhalation in a churchyard thought to presage death.

XVIII

Here Jack and Tom are pair'd with Moll and Meg.
Curved open to the river-reach is seen
A country merry-making on the green.
Fair space for signal shakings of the leg.
That little screwy fiddler from his booth,
Whence flows one nut-brown stream, commands
    the joints
Of all who caper here at various points.
I have known rustic revels in my youth:
The May-fly pleasures of a mind at ease.
An early goddess was a country lass:
A charm'd Amphion-oak[14] she tripped the grass.
What life was that I lived? The life of these?
God keep them happy! Nature they are near.
They must, I think, be wiser than I am:
They have the secret of the bull and lamb.
'Tis true that when we trace its source, 'tis beer.

14 *Amphion*: Amphion's lyre could draw stones after him.

XIX

No state is enviable. To the luck alone
Of some few favour'd men I would put claim.
I bleed, but she who wounds I will not blame.
Have I not felt her heart as 'twere my own,
Beat thro' me? could I hurt her? Heaven and Hell!
But I could hurt her cruelly! Can I let
My Love's old time-piece to another set,
Swear it can't stop, and must for ever swell?
Sure, that's one way Love drifts into the mart
Where goat-legg'd buyers[15] throng. I see not
    plain: —
My meaning is, it must not be again.
Great God! the maddest gambler throws his heart.
If any state be enviable on earth,
'Tis yon born idiot's, who, as days go by,
Still rubs his hands before him like a fly,
In a queer sort of meditative mirth.

15 *goat-legg'd buyers*: centaurs, half-man, half-goat, signify lust.

X X

I am not of those miserable males
Who sniff at vice, and, daring not to snap,
Do therefore hope for Heaven. I take the hap
Of all my deeds. The wind that fills my sails,
Propels; but I am helmsman. Am I wreck'd,
I know the devil has sufficient weight
To bear: I lay it not on him, or fate.
Besides, he's damn'd. That man I do suspect
A coward, who would burden the poor deuce
With what ensues from his own slipperiness.
I have just found a wanton-scented tress
In an old desk, dusty for lack of use.
Of days and nights it is demonstrative,
That like a blasted star gleam luridly.
If for that time I must ask charity,
Have I not any charity to give?

XXI

We three are on the cedar-shadow'd lawn;
My friend being third. He who at love once
    laugh'd,
Is in the weak rib by a fatal shaft
Struck through and tells his passion's bashful dawn,
And radiant culmination, glorious crown,
When 'this' she said: went 'thus': most wondrous
    she!
Our eyes grow white, encountering; that we are
    three,
Forgetful; then together we look down.
But he demands our blessing; is convinced
That words of wedded lovers must bring good.
We question: if we dare! or if we should!
And pat him, with light laugh. We have not
    winced.
Next, she has fallen. Fainting points the sign[16]
To happy things in wedlock. When she wakes
She looks the star that thro' the cedar shakes:
Her lost moist hand clings mortally to mine.

---

16 *Fainting points the sign*: but she is not pregnant.

XXII

What may this woman labour to confess?
There is about her mouth a nervous twitch.
'Tis something to be told, or hidden: – which?
I get a glimpse of Hell in this mild guess.
She has desires of touch, as if to feel
That all the household things are things she knew.
She stops before the glass. What does she view?
A face that seems the latest to reveal!
For she turns from it hastily, and toss'd
Irresolute, steals shadow-like to where
I stand; and wavering pale before me there,
Her tears fall still as oak-leaves after frost.
She will not speak. I will not ask. We are
League-sunder'd by the silent gulf between.
You burly lovers on the village green,
Yours is a lower, but a happier star!

XXIII

'Tis Christmas weather, and a country house
Receives us: rooms are full: we can but get
An attic-crib. Such lovers will not fret
At that, it is half-said. The great carouse
Knocks hard upon the midnight's hollow door.
But when I knock at hers, I see the pit.
Why did I come here in that dullard fit?
I enter, and lie couch'd upon the floor.
Passing, I caught the coverlid's quick beat: –
Come, Shame, burn to my soul! and Pride, and
    Pain –
Foul demons that have tortured me, sustain!
Out in the freezing darkness the lambs bleat.
The small bird stiffens in the low starlight.
I know not how, but, shuddering as I slept,
I dream'd a banish'd Angel to me crept:
My feet[17] were nourish'd on her breasts all night.

17 *my feet*: head to toe, intimate and alienated.

XXIV

The misery is greater, as I live!
To know her flesh so pure, so keen her sense,
That she does penance now for no offence,
Save against Love. The less can I forgive!
The less can I forgive, though I adore
That cruel lovely pallor which surrounds
Her footsteps; and the low vibrating sounds
That come on me, as from a magic shore.
Low are they, but most subtle to find out
The shrinking soul. Madam, 'tis understood
When women play upon their womanhood.
It means, a Season gone. And yet I doubt
But I am duped. That nun-like look waylays
My fancy. Oh! I do but wait a sign!
Pluck out the eyes of Pride! thy mouth to mine!
Never! though I die thirsting. Go thy ways!

XXV

You like not that French novel? Tell me why.
You think it most unnatural. Let us see.
The actors are, it seems, the usual three:
Husband, and wife, and lover. She – but fie!
In England we'll not hear of it. Edmond,
The lover, her devout chagrin doth share;
Blanc-mange and absinthe are his penitent fare,
Till his pale aspect makes her overfond:
So, to preclude fresh sin, he tries rosbif.
Meantime the husband is no more abused:
Auguste forgives her ere the tear is used.
Then hangeth all on one tremendous If:–
IF she will choose between them! She does choose;
And takes her husband like a proper wife.
Unnatural? My dear, these things are life:
And life, they say, is worthy of the Muse.

XXVI

Love ere he bleeds, an eagle in high skies,
Has earth beneath his wings: from redden'd eve
He views the rosy dawn. In vain they weave
The fatal web below while far he flies.
But when the arrow strikes him, there's a change.
He moves but in the track of his spent pain,
Whose red drops are the links of a harsh chain,
Binding him to the ground with narrow range.
A subtle serpent then has Love become.
I had the eagle in my bosom erst.
Henceforward with the serpent I am curs'd.
I can interpret where the mouth is dumb.
Speak, and I see the side-lie of a truth.
Perchance my heart may pardon you this deed:
But be no coward:– you that made Love bleed,
You must bear all the venom of his tooth!

XXVII

Distraction is the panacea, Sir!
I hear my Oracle of Medicine say.
Doctor! that same specific yesterday
I tried, and the result will not deter
A second trial. Is the devil's line
Of golden hair, or raven black, composed?
And does a cheek, like any sea-shell rosed,
Or fair as widow'd Heaven, seem most divine?
No matter, so I taste forgetfulness.
And if the devil snare me, body and mind,
Here gratefully I score:– he seemèd kind,
When not a soul would comfort my distress!
O sweet new world in which I rise new made!
O Lady, once I gave love: now I take!
Lady, I must be flatter'd. Shouldst thou wake
The passion of a demon, be not afraid.

XXVIII

I must be flatter'd. The imperious
Desire speaks out. Lady, I am content
To play with you the game of Sentiment,
And with you enter on paths perilous:
But if across your beauty I throw light,
To make it threefold, it must be all mine.
First secret; then avow'd. For I must shine
Envied, – I, lessen'd in my proper sight!
Be watchful of your beauty, Lady dear!
How much hangs on that lamp you cannot tell.
Most earnestly I pray you, tend it well:
And men shall see me like the burning sphere:
And men shall mark you eyeing me, and groan
To be the God of such a grand sunflower!
I feel the promptings of Satanic power,
While you do homage unto me alone.

XXIX

Am I failing? for no longer can I cast
A glory round about this head of gold.
Glory she wears, but springing from the mould:
Not like the consecration of the Past!
Is my soul beggar'd? Something more than earth
I cry for still: I cannot be at peace
In having Love upon a mortal lease.
I cannot take the woman at her worth!
Where is the ancient wealth wherewith I clothed
Our human nakedness, and could endow
With spiritual splendour a white brow
That else had grinn'd at me the fact I loath'd?
A kiss is but a kiss now! and no wave
Of a great flood that whirls me to the sea.
But, as you will! we'll sit contentedly,
And eat our pot of honey on the grave.

XXX

What are we first? First, animals; and next,
Intelligences at a leap; on whom
Pale lies the distant shadow of the tomb,
And all that draweth on the tomb for text.
Into this state comes Love, the crowning sun:
Beneath whose light the shadow loses form.
We are the lords of life, and life is warm.
Intelligence and instinct now are one.
But Nature says: 'My children most they seem
When they least know me: therefore I decree
That they shall suffer.' Swift doth young Love flee:
And we stand waken'd, shivering from our dream.
Then if we study Nature we are wise.
Thus do the few who live but with the day.
The scientific animals are they. –
Lady, this is my Sonnet to your eyes.[18]

18 cf. Shakespeare's satirical sonnet 130: 'My mistress' eyes are
nothing like the sun'.

XXXI

This golden head has wit in it. I live
Again, and a far higher life, near her.
Some women like a young philosopher;
Perchance because he is diminutive.
For woman's manly god must not exceed
Proportions of the natural nursing size.
Great poets and great sages draw no prize
With women: but the little lap–dog breed,
Who can be hugg'd, or on a mantel–piece
Perch'd up for adoration, these obtain
Her homage. And of this we men are vain?
Of this! 'Tis order'd for the world's increase!
Small flattery! Yet she has that rare gift
To beauty, Common Sense. I am approved.
It is not half so nice as being loved,
And yet I do prefer it. What's my drift?

XXXII

Full faith I have she holds that rarest gift
To beauty, Common Sense. To see her lie
With her fair visage an inverted sky
Bloom-cover'd, while the underlids uplift,
Would almost wreck the faith; but when her mouth
(Can it kiss sweetly? sweetly!) would address
The inner me that thirsts for her no less,
And has so long been languishing in drouth,
I feel that I am match'd: that I am man!
One restless corner of my heart, or head,
That holds a dying something never dead,
Still frets, though Nature giveth all she can.
It means, that woman is not, I opine,
Her sex's antidote. Who seeks the asp[19]
For serpents' bites? 'Twould calm me could I clasp
Shrieking Bacchantes[20] with their souls of wine!

19 *Who seeks the asp*: the asp that killed Cleopatra was a serpent; i.e. fire does not drive out fire, there is no antidote to loving his wife in wooing another woman.

20 *Shrieking Bacchantes*: the orgiastic might calm him, Common Sense cannot.

XXXIII

'In Paris, at the Louvre,²¹ there have I seen
The sumptuously-feather'd angel pierce
Prone Lucifer, descending. Look'd he fierce,
Showing the fight a fair one? Too serene!
The young Pharsalians did not disarray
Less willingly their locks of floating silk:
That suckling mouth of his, upon the milk
Of stars might still be feasting through the fray.
Oh, Raphael! when men the Fiend do fight,
They conquer not upon such easy terms.
Half serpent in the struggle grow these worms.
And does he grow half human, all is right.'
This to my Lady in a distant spot,
Upon the theme: '*While mind is mastering clay,
Gross clay invades it.*' If the spy you play,
My wife, read this! Strange love-talk, is it not?

21 *at the Louvre:* Raphael pictures a tranquil and unruffled angel, as
smooth as the young Romans who did not want to disarrange
their hair at the Battle of Pharsalia: in real life the struggle with
evil makes men themselves half-devils.

XXXIV

Madam would speak with me. So, now it comes:
The Deluge, or else Fire! She's well; she thanks
My husbandship. Our chain through silence clanks.
Time leers between us, twiddling his thumbs.
Am I quite well? Most excellent in health!
The journals, too, I diligently peruse.
Vesuvius is expected to give news:
Niagara is no noisier. By stealth
Our eyes dart scrutinizing snakes. She's glad
I'm happy, says her quivering under-lip.
'And are not you?' 'How can I be?' 'Take ship!
For happiness is somewhere to be had.'
'Nowhere for me!' Her voice is barely heard.
I am not melted, and make no pretence.
With truisms I freeze her, tongue and sense.
Niagara, or Vesuvius, is deferr'd.

XXXV

It is no vulgar nature I have wived.
Secretive, sensitive, she takes a wound
Deep to her soul, as if the sense had swoon'd,
And not a thought of vengeance had survived.
No confidences has she: but relief
Must come to one whose suffering is acute.
O have a care of natures that are mute!
They punish you in acts: their steps are brief.
What is she doing? What does she demand
From Providence, or me? She is not one
Long to endure this torpidly, and shun
The drugs that crowd about a woman's hand.
At Forfeits during snow we play'd, and I
Must kiss her. 'Well perform'd!' I said: then she:
''Tis hardly worth the money, you agree?'
Save her? What for? To act this wedded lie!

XXXVI

My Lady unto Madam makes her bow.
The charm of women is, that even while
You're probed by them for tears, you yet may
    smile,
Nay, laugh outright, as I have done just now.
The interview was gracious: they anoint
(To me aside) each other with fine praise:
Discriminating compliments they raise,
That hit with wondrous aim on the weak point.
My Lady's nose of nature might complain.
It is not fashion'd aptly to express
Her character of large-brow'd stedfastness.
But Madam says: Thereof she may be vain!
Now, Madam's faulty feature is a glazed
And inaccessible eye, that has soft fires,
Wide gates, at love-time only. This admires
My Lady. At the two I stand amazed.

XXXVII

Along the garden terrace, under which
A purple valley (lighted at its edge
By smoky torch-flame on the long cloud-ledge
Whereunder dropp'd the chariot), glimmers rich,
A quiet company we pace, and wait
The dinner-bell in pre-digestive calm.
So sweet up violet banks the Southern balm[22]
Breathes round, we care not if the bell be late:
Tho' here and there gray seniors question Time
In irritable coughings. With slow foot
The low, rosed moon, the face of Music mute,
Begins among her silent bars to climb.
As in and out, in silvery dusk, we thread,
I hear the laugh of Madam, and discern
My Lady's heel before me at each turn.
Our Tragedy, is it alive or dead?

22 *So sweet up violet banks the Southern balm*: compare Lorenzo's
speech in *The Merchant of Venice* on a similarly tranquil evening.

XXXVIII

Give to imagination some pure light
In human form to fix it, or you shame
The devils with that hideous human game:–
Imagination urging appetite!
Thus fallen have earth's greatest Gogmagogs,[23]
Who dazzle us, whom we cannot revere.
Imagination is the charioteer
That, in default of better, drives the hogs.
So, therefore, my dear Lady, let me love!
My soul is arrow'd to the light in you.
You know me that I never can renew
The bond that woman broke: what would you
    have?
'Tis Love, or Vileness! not a choice between,
Save petrifaction! What does Pity here?
She kill'd a thing, and now it's dead, 'tis dear.
O, when you counsel me, think what you mean!

23 *Gogmagogs*: one of the twelve-foot giants who originally inhab-
ited Britain; he was defeated and thrown into the sea.

XXXIX

She yields: my Lady in her noblest mood
Has yielded: she, my golden-crownëd rose!
The bride of every sense! more sweet than those
Who breathe the violet breath of maidenhood.
O visage of still music in the sky!
Soft moon! I feel thy song, my fairest friend!
True harmony within can apprehend
Dumb harmony without. And hark! 'tis nigh!
Belief has struck the note of sound: a gleam
Of living silver shows me where she shook
Her long white fingers down the shadowy brook,
That sings her song, half waking, half in dream.
What two come here to mar this heavenly tune?
A man is one: the woman bears my name,
And honour. Their hands touch! Am I still tame?
God, what a dancing spectre seems the moon!

XL

I bade my Lady think what she might mean.
Know I my meaning, *I*? Can I love one,
And yet be jealous of another? None
Commit such folly. Terrible Love, I ween,
Has might, even dead, half sighing to upheave
The lightless seas of selfishness amain:
Seas that in a man's heart have no rain
To fall and still them. Peace can I achieve
By turning to this fountain-source of woe,
This woman, who's to Love as fire to wood?
She breath'd the violet breath of maidenhood
Against my kisses once! but I say, No!
The thing is mock'd at! Helplessly afloat,
I know not what I do, whereto I strive.
The dread that my old love may be alive,
Has seiz'd my nursling new love by the throat.

XLI

How many a thing which we cast to the ground,
When others pick it up becomes a gem!
We grasp at all the wealth it is to them;
And by reflected light its worth is found.
Yet for us still 'tis nothing! and that zeal
Of false appreciation quickly fades.
This truth is little known to human shades,
How rare from their own instinct 'tis to feel!
They waste the soul with spurious desire,
That is not the ripe flame upon the bough:
We two have taken up a lifeless vow
To rob a living passion: dust for fire!
Madam is grave, and eyes the clock that tells
Approaching midnight. We have struck despair
Into two hearts. O, look we like a pair
Who for fresh nuptials joyfully yield all else?

XLII

I am to follow her. There is much grace
In women when thus bent on martyrdom.
They think that dignity of soul may come,
Perchance, with dignity of body. Base!
But I was taken by that air of cold
And statuesque sedateness, when she said,
'I'm going;' lit the taper, bow'd her head,
And went, as with the stride of Pallas bold.[24]
Fleshly indifference horrible! The hands
Of Time now signal: O, she's safe from me!
Within those secret walls what do I see?
Where first she set the taper down she stands:
Not Pallas: Hebe shamed![25] Thoughts black as death,
Like a stirr'd pool in sunshine break. Her wrists
I catch: she faltering, as she half resists,
'You love . . .? love . . .? love . . .?' all in an indrawn
    breath.

---

24 *Pallas bold*: Pallas Athena sprang forth full-grown from the
head of Zeus, confident and uttering her war-cry.
25 *Hebe shamed*: the cup-bearer or servitor of the gods. The wife
shifts from assurance to anxiety: does he love her or another
woman?

XLIII

Mark where the pressing wind shoots javelin-like,
Its skeleton shadow on the broad-back'd wave!
Here is a fitting spot to dig Love's grave;
Here where the ponderous breakers plunge and strike,
And dart their hissing tongues high up the sand:
In hearing of the ocean, and in sight
Of those ribb'd wind-streaks running into white.
If I the death of Love had deeply plann'd,
I never could have made it half so sure,
As by the unbless'd kisses which upbraid
The full-waked sense; or, failing that, degrade!
'Tis morning: but no morning can restore
What we have forfeited. I see no sin:
The wrong is mix'd. In tragic life, God wot,
No villain need be! Passions spin the plot:
We are betray'd by what is false within.

XLIV

They say that Pity in Love's service dwells,
A porter at the rosy temple's gate.
I miss'd him going: but it is my fate
To come upon him now beside his wells;
Whereby I know that I Love's temple leave,
And that the purple doors have closed behind.
Poor soul! if in those early days unkind,
Thy power to sting had been but power to grieve,
We now might with an equal spirit meet,
And not be match'd like innocence and vice.
She for the Temple's worship has paid price,
And takes the coin of Pity as a cheat.
She sees thro' simulation to the bone:
What's best in her impels her to the worst.
Never, she cries, shall Pity soothe Love's thirst,
Or foul hypocrisy for truth atone!

XLV

It is the season of the sweet wild rose,
My Lady's emblem in the heart of me!
So golden-crownëd shines she gloriously,
And with that softest dream of blood she glows:
Mild as an evening Heaven round Hesper bright!
I pluck the flower, and smell it, and revive
The time when in her eyes I stood alive.
I seem to look upon it out of Night.
Here's Madam, stepping hastily. Her whims
Bid her demand the flower, which I let drop.
As I proceed, I feel her sharply stop,
And crush it under heel with trembling limbs.
She joins me in a cat-like way, and talks
Of company, and even condescends
To utter laughing scandal of old friends.
These are the summer days, and these our walks.

XLVI

At last we parley: we so strangely dumb
In such a close communion! It befell
About the sounding of the Matin-bell,
And lo! her place was vacant, and the hum
Of loneliness was round me. Then I rose,
And my disorder'd brain did guide my foot
To that old wood where our first love-salute
Was interchanged: the source of many throes!
There did I see her, not alone. I moved
Towards her, and made proffer of my arm.
She took it simply, with no rude alarm;
And that disturbing shadow pass'd reproved.
I felt the pain'd speech coming, and declared
My firm belief in her, ere she could speak.
A ghastly morning came into her cheek,
While with a widening soul on me she stared.

XLVII

We saw the swallows gathering in the sky,
And in the osier-isle we heard their noise.
We had not to look back on summer joys,
Or forward to a summer of bright dye.
But in the largeness of the evening earth
Our spirits grew as we went side by side.
The hour became her husband, and my bride.
Love that had robb'd us so, thus bless'd our dearth!
The pilgrims of the year wax'd very loud
In multitudinous chatterings, as the flood
Full brown came from the west, and like pale blood
Expanded to the upper crimson cloud.
Love that had robb'd us of immortal things,
This little moment mercifully gave,
And still I see across the twilight wave,
The swan sail with her young beneath her wings.

XLVIII

Their sense is with their senses all mix'd in.
Destroy'd by subtleties these women are!
More brain, O Lord, more brain! or we shall mar
Utterly this fair garden we might win.
Behold! I looked for peace, and thought it near.
Our inmost hearts had open'd, each to each.
We drank the pure daylight of honest speech.
Alas! that was the fatal draught, I fear.
For when of my lost Lady came the word,
This woman, O this agony of flesh!
Jealous devotion bade her break the mesh,
That I might seek that other like a bird.
I do adore the nobleness! despise
The act! She has gone forth, I know not where.
Will the hard world my sentience of her share?
I feel the truth; so let the world surmise.

XLIX

He found her by the ocean's moaning verge,
Nor any wicked change in her discern'd;
And she believed his old love had return'd,
Which was her exultation, and her scourge.
She took his hand, and walked with him, and
    seem'd
The wife he sought, tho' shadowlike and dry.
She had one terror, lest her heart should sigh,
And tell her loudly she no longer dream'd.
She dared not say, 'This is my breast: look in.'
But there's a strength to help the desperate weak.
That night he learnt how silence best can speak
The awful things when Pity pleads for Sin.
About the middle of the night her call
Was heard, and he came wondering to the bed.
'Now kiss me, dear! it may be, now!' she said.
Lethe had pass'd those lips, and he knew all.

L

Thus piteously Love closed what he begat:
The union of this ever-diverse pair!
These two were rapid falcons in a snare,
Condemn'd to do the flitting of the bat.
Lovers beneath the singing sky of May,
They wander'd once; clear as the dew on flowers:
But they fed not on the advancing hours:
Their hearts held cravings for the buried day.
Then each applied to each that fatal knife,
Deep questioning, which probes to endless dole.
Ah, what a dusty answer gets the soul
When hot for certainties in this our life! –
In tragic hints here see what evermore
Moves dark as yonder midnight ocean's force,
Thundering like ramping hosts of warrior horse,
To throw that faint thin line upon the shore!

This edition follows the first edition: *Modern Love and Poems of the English Roadside with Poems and Ballads*, Chapman and Hall, 1862. An introductory poem, 'The Promise in Disturbance', was added when the sequence was reprinted in 1892 (see P. Bartlett (ed.) *Poems*, Yale University Press, p. 115).